Tyler's Purple Arm

Amanda Donahue

Illustrated by Mat Sadler

For Tyler

You are genuine, kind, loving, and brave.
Thank you for letting me share your story.

— Amanda

TYLER'S PURPLE ARM

Text and illustrations copyright © Amanda Jo Donahue, 2022
All rights reserved

Library of Congress Control Number: 2022916701

Hardcover ISBN: 979-8-9857649-2-5
Paperback ISBN: 979-8-9857649-1-8
Digital ISBN: 979-8-9857649-0-1

In a school full of children
with skin of all tones,
a student named Tyler
stood out on his own.

He was born with two arms,
both a left and a right,
but with one colored purple
and one colored white.

A birthmark,
it's called,
some are
born with this
hue.

Like your hair, nose, and eyes,
it helps make you, YOU!

Birthmarks aren't bad,
they're not gross or contagious.
If you see one, don't stare—
just ask! Be courageous!

But when little Tyler
began at his school,
he sadly soon learned
that some kids can be cruel.

They stared and they pointed.
They laughed at his arm.
They did NOT see his smile
or notice his charm.

Some children were mean
with their whispers and cries.
But he chose to be brave
and to hold his head high.

Yes, purple is different,
but different's not bad!
He was raised to believe
life's too short to be sad.

He liked his uniqueness
and wore a big grin.
He loved to teach others
we are more than our skin.

His approach soon rubbed off.
"What birthmark?" they'd say.
No one noticed it now
when they asked him to play.

It's what's inside that counts,
how we treat one another.
Tyler lived this wise truth
and saw good in each brother...

...each sister, each teacher,
each bully, and friend.
His kind words and deeds
soon began a new trend.

With love and compassion
for each person's gifts,
Tyler led by example
and helped their minds shift.

His purple arm worked,
and his hand sure did, too!
He could juggle and type
and climb trees just like you!

He loved football
and tennis,
played soccer,
ran track.

He beat video games—
not a thing held him
back!

Tyler proudly made music
on trumpet in band.
Every trophy he won,
he held high with that hand.

Brave Tyler soon taught
all the people he knew,
that our skin doesn't limit
what things we can do.

Your skin's just a cover
of what's underneath.

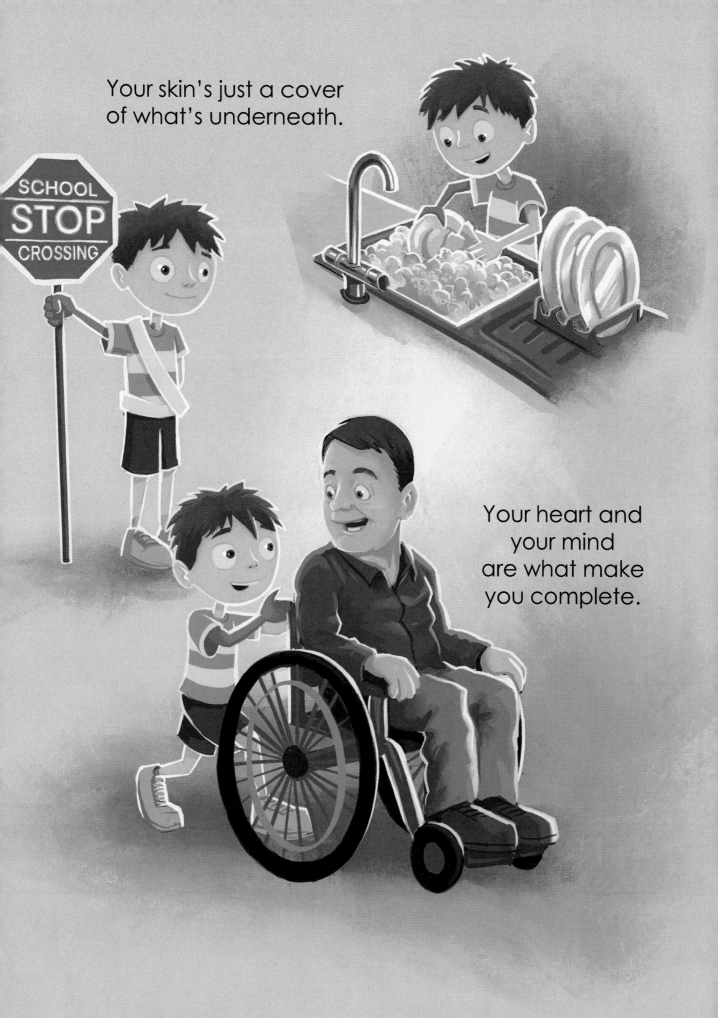

Your heart and
your mind
are what make
you complete.

For under that birthmark
inside this wise boy,
a loving heart beat
with acceptance and joy.

Birthmarks add color
in all shapes and all shades.
Tyler helped us to see
how uniquely we're made!

It's what's inside that counts,
not the skin that we have.
Yes, purple is different.
But different's not bad.

Amanda Donahue's background as an educator of young children, along with having five kids of her own, has exposed her to a broad spectrum of children's books over the years, yet none that involved a child character with a birthmark. Amanda was inspired to write her story after visiting her children's classrooms with her husband, Tyler, who was born with Klippel-Trenaunay Syndrome (KTS) which produced a port-wine stain (purple birthmark) on his right arm. Backed by the advice and support of Tyler's doctor at the Mayo Clinic, Amanda was able to create a story that celebrates uniqueness, kindness, and acceptance. Her heartwarming story normalizes skin differences while teaching kids about them in the process, providing a poignant resource for families and educators.

Amanda graduated Magna Cum Laude from Illinois Wesleyan University, where she majored in Educational Studies and minored in Psychology. She lives with her husband, Tyler, and their five boys in Central Illinois. *Tyler's Purple Arm* is her debut picture book.

Mat Sadler's illustrations helped create the stunning backdrop to *Tyler's Purple Arm*. His use of bright, cheerful colors captures the eye and artfully conveys the positive imagery for this inspiring story. With extraordinary attention given to the details that make us each unique, while celebrating our physical differences, *Tyler's Purple Arm* is a visual delight with an uplifting message.

Mat lives in Brentwood, Essex in the United Kingdom, and is the married father of two children. Mat studied Fine Art at Aberystwyth University. In addition to *Tyler's Purple Arm*, he has illustrated numerous children's books.

Made in United States
Orlando, FL
05 December 2022

25517005R10015